Trading Riley

Mar'ce Merrell

Trading Riley

Mar'ce Merrell

Cover by Kristine Makauskas

ROUSSAN
PUBLISHERS INC.
Specializing in YA and fiction for pre-teens
MONTRÉAL

THE CANADA COUNCIL | LE CONSEIL DES ARTS
FOR THE ARTS | DU CANADA
SINCE 1957 | DEPUIS 1957

We acknowledge the support of the Canada Council for the Arts
for our publishing program.

We acknowledge the financial support of the Government of Canada
through the Book Publishing Industry Development Program
for publishing activities.

http://www.roussan.com

National Library of Canada
Bibliothèque nationale du Québec

National Library of Canada Cataloguing in Publication Data

Merrell, Mar'ce, 1966-
Trading Riley

Age 8-11.
ISBN 1-896184-88-X

I. Title.

PS8576.E738T73 2001   jC813'.54   C2001-900357-9

PZ7.M47Tr 2001

$6.95

J P B
M E R
C . 1

Cover by Kristine Makauskas
Graphics by Gregory de Roussan
Interior design by Jean Shepherd
Perpetua

Published simultaneously in Canada and the United States of America
Printed in Canada

1 2 3 4 5 6 7 8 9 UTP 9 8 7 6 5 4 3 2 1

For Andrew and Chris who have endured a
gopher museum and a whole lot more...
Thank you. And to D.S., a fellow stepmom.

Thank you to my family, Dennis, Andrew,
Callie, Chris, Cam, Ben, and friend
Celeste, for your encouragement.

Thank you to Alison Lohans for nurturing
and nudging this story. Thank you to
Carmen, Jocelyn, Colleen and Rod
who read earlier drafts of the work.

 1
Scared Lizards

"They look scared," Riley said as he peered into his lizard's cage. Lizzy and Megarra, usually curled on the rocks in the sunshine, hung upside down from the screen ceiling. They were waiting, just like Riley, for his almost-stepmom Debbie to complete her makeup ritual before they could leave the driveway.

"Scared? How can lizards be scared?" Debbie glided a tube of coffee-colored lipstick along her bottom lip. Riley watched as she smooshed her lips together.

"Lizards have many enemies. They're nearly at the bottom of the food chain. Look at their color and the way they're hanging at the top of the cage, they are definitely scared."

"You're kidding, right?" Debbie turned to him. He could see himself in her shiny black sunglasses. His mouth was in a thin, straight line. He pushed his glasses up to his face.

"Okay, you're not kidding. What's wrong with them, then?" Debbie pulled her sunglasses down her nose and stared at Riley. She looked like a movie star on her way to the mall to sign autographs, not a stepmom who was going camping for four days.

"The lizards are scared because…" Riley looked out the window, searching for a way to explain. "This is a strange environment. They're not used to it. They're not used to you."

"Well, there's nothing we can do about me. I'm the driver. And I can't see how they'd be afraid of this car; practically everything you own is stuffed in here." Debbie opened the glove compartment and fished out the maps Riley and his dad had gotten when they were planning the trip.

Riley watched his neighbor's dog lift his leg and pee on the planter full of yellow and purple pansies that stood next to the driveway. They'd never had planters before Debbie came. Riley wondered if the dog just liked the planter or if it was the location of the planter that was most important.

"We could always leave the lizards at home," Debbie announced. "My sister will feed them."

"We're not leaving Lizzy and Megarra with a stranger," Riley said through clenched teeth.

"You'll be home in three weeks. They'll be fine." Debbie chewed her thumbnail. Flakes of chocolate nail polish fell onto her cream-colored pants.

"They're my pets. They go where I go. They always have." Riley had wanted a dog but his parents told him dogs didn't live too well in two different houses. Lizards, they said, could be traded with no problems. And they did, until Debbie got involved. Riley heard the grinding of a semi-trailer and an ambulance siren blaring. He closed his eyes and took a deep breath.

"I sure wish your dad were here."

"That makes four of us," Riley spit out. Dad had set up the

camping trip to cheer Riley up once he heard that Mom could only take him for three weeks; Debbie wasn't even going to go. Then Dad's best friend from college died in a car accident. Dad had left for the funeral only a few hours ago.

"Four of us? There's just you and me."

"What about Lizzy and Megarra? You don't think they want Dad, too?" Riley's face felt hot.

Debbie chewed on her bottom lip as she stared out the window. "First we had to get everything you owned from your bedroom for a three-week vacation. Then we have this: the lizards are scared!"

Riley leaned his head against the window. He stared at the elm trees with the yellow stickered trunks that lined the street. STOP THE SPREAD OF ELM DISEASE. He still didn't know how those stickers were going to help, but he'd stuck them on all the same. It seemed like a good idea.

"What do you want to do, Riley? Do you want to stay here in the driveway? Do you want to unpack everything and wait for your dad to come back in a week? Or do you want me to get you to your mom's place?" Riley's neck itched at the anger in Debbie's voice.

"I want to go," Riley whispered. He knew it was his only choice. If he stayed and waited for Dad, he would have one less week with Mom.

"Good!" Debbie fluffed her hair with her chocolate-colored talons.

"About the lizards," Riley said slowly.

"Yes?" Debbie asked.

"They just need one thing. It's something that's always next to their cage. I think it will help."

"Well," Debbie hesitated. "Okay, go get it."

"I'll be right back." Riley jumped out of the car, unlocked the front door and ran to his bedroom. He returned to the driveway carrying Rufus, a stuffed animal who usually sat next to the lizard cage in his room.

"This is what the lizards need," he said. The stuffed dog hit the pavement with a thud. It was nearly as tall as Riley.

"This?" Debbie asked. Rufus' long red tongue lapped at the dirt on the driveway. In his backpack, Riley had a picture taken the day Dad won Rufus with the whole family, Mom included, at Klondike days. Before the divorce.

"They want a guard dog. It's going to be four days with camping in strange places and with—" Riley almost said "strange people" but he stopped himself.

Debbie raised her eyebrows, looking through the back window of the car. Riley followed her eyes. A jumble of shapes and colors fought for space. It would be difficult to fit a can of pop in there.

"You can see the car, Riley. There's nowhere for it to go. It just won't fit." Debbie scratched the side of her nose.

"He has to." Now that Rufus was down here, Riley wouldn't take him back.

"Lizards," Debbie sighed. She frowned at Rufus.

"Well, let's see how we can get this in, then." Debbie smiled, but just a little. Riley smiled, too. He had won.

Riley buckled his seat belt and laid his head back, squinting against the hot sunshine. He couldn't think of anything more to bring. They would be leaving now. He felt his stomach begin to ache.

I'm more like a dog than a lizard. I don't get traded very well, either.

2
Tricked Lizards

"How are those little critters doing?" Debbie had turned the radio down to talk to Riley.

Riley looked back. Lizzy was stretched out on a rock, soaking in the sunlight from the open sunroof. Megarra was hiding under the pointy, deep green leaves of the plant Dad had added to the lizard cage last summer. The lizards were now a bright green color, the color of algae in a fish tank.

"Okay," Riley answered. "They're green." He tilted his head back, watching streaks of clouds zooming through endless blue sky.

"Green?" Debbie's glasses flashed at him. "Oh no. Don't tell me they're sick!"

"Debbie, these are *Anole* lizards. They change from brown to green and green to brown all the time. That's partly how they warm up and cool off." Riley pushed his glasses farther up. They were always falling down. "Green means they're warm and calm." Debbie turned back to the road, drumming her fingers on the wheel.

"Hey!" Debbie hit the steering wheel. Riley jerked up in his seat. "Come on, buddy, there's two lanes on this road," Debbie pleaded to the driver in the car in front of them. "Pick one!" She honked her horn. Riley caught a blur of an old blue truck with rust holes as they passed.

Debbie turned the radio up full blast and started to sing. Lizzy ran for cover under the plant leaves next to Megarra. Riley stared out the window. Driving fast was good; it would be over quicker that way. Bright yellow canola fields swayed in the wind, waving goodbye.

WESTASKIWIN. PONOKA. LACOMBE. Riley read the signs and listened to Debbie singing. Every song they played. When she didn't know the words, she sang la, la, la. She even sang the radio jingles, "QRXZ, Today's Best Music!" Her white teeth shone in the sunlight.

Riley unfolded the map of Alberta. He found the green circle around Edmonton and followed with his finger to the last sign he had seen, RED DEER.

"An inch!" he complained. "We've been driving all this time and we've only traveled an inch!" Debbie turned down the radio.

"It sure seems long, doesn't it?" she said. "But don't worry. When I was going through the maps last night, I noticed you and your dad hadn't planned any stops along the way to kind of break up the trip. So I've got a little surprise for you." She showed Riley her full-teeth smile.

"I don't like surprises," Riley said, which was partially true. He liked surprises when Dad said they could go for ice cream after dinner. But not surprises like, *Debbie and I are getting married next Christmas.* Dad had made that announcement a couple of weeks before he suggested the camping trip.

"You'll like this surprise, Riley," Debbie said.

12

"What is it?" Riley wanted to know.

"Oh! This is our exit." Debbie leaned on the brakes and pulled off the highway. Riley lurched forward in the seat. She turned at the sign that read OLDS, TROCHU, TORRINGTON.

"What do you mean, our exit?" Riley said. "We're supposed to stay on Highway 2 until we get to Airdrie." Riley had the route memorized. His dad told him last night when he was tucking him in that Riley had to be a good navigator. "Debbie gets a little mixed up about what direction she's headed," Dad had laughed. "There's a reason she's got a compass on her dashboard."

Riley looked at the bobbing compass on the dash. It pointed east.

"Uh Debbie, the compass says we're going east. We should be going west." Debbie kept driving. They passed more canola fields and white farmhouses with porches and swings and big rocking chairs.

"Why are you changing the plans?" Riley shifted in his seat, kicking the sleeping bag at his feet. He heard the lizards moving in their cage. He glanced back at them. Lizzy was climbing up the side, his toes gripping the slick glass. He looked like he wanted to get out.

"Riley, this is no longer your trip with your dad. It's a trip with me. I wanted to surprise you. I think you'll really love this place." Debbie's hands gripped the steering wheel. "Your dad thought it was a good idea, too."

That was all Riley needed to hear. He shut his mouth. Riley had read a book about a bad stepmother, several books. Debbie was already getting Dad to gang up on him.

The sun blazed through the windshield. Riley was boiling hot. He wanted to roll down the window but that would have meant asking Debbie if it was okay. He shut his eyes and thought about Mom.

He could predict some of the things they'd do. First they'd stay up till two a.m. each night to watch the movies she helped make; she was a camera operator and worked on TV shows, movies. Then they'd sleep in late and go to the beach to paint watercolors and go swimming. The car stopped just as Riley was imagining what kind of vegetarian food Mom would make for dinner. He opened his eye closest to the window.

A gopher was staring at him. It was bigger than Mr. Fine, his school principal who could touch the basketball net if he stood on his toes. They came here to see a statue of a gopher dressed in a straw hat and overalls? TORRINGTON, LITTLE VILLAGE ON THE PRAIRIE, read the sign at the gopher's feet.

Debbie turned at the only gas station and traveled down a street past ten small houses. "Hm. I thought the sign said it was on this street," she mumbled. "It must be one over. I hate getting lost."

"Uh… Debbie? You mean we're lost in Torrington? The little village on the prairie? Population 200?" Riley laughed. Debbie sighed. She was mad. Again.

"Here we are." Debbie smiled. "The World Famous Gopher Hole Museum." The car crawled to a stop on the gravel driveway next to a small trailer like the ones on construction sites.

"This is the surprise?" Riley studied the gopher painted on the trailer.

"Isn't it great? I know how much you like little critters like Lizzy and Dizzy, there." Debbie pointed to the back seat.

"Their names are Lizzy and Megarra," Riley corrected her. She couldn't remember their names. She didn't even care about them, did she? "Lizards are reptiles, not critters. Gophers are rodents. I'm not interested in rodents."

"Well, maybe you just don't know if you're interested. I read about this place in the paper. It's supposed to be very good." Debbie searched through her purse. She pulled out her lipstick. "They've got displays of stuffed gophers. Even a couple of rare black ones."

"Stuffed? You mean the gophers are DEAD?" Riley stared at her. He loved animals. He'd even been thinking he wanted to be an animal trainer for movies. Maybe he'd make a movie with Mom about lizards who got left behind when their family moved and they found their way back.

"Well...yes...they're stuffed. You know, by a taxidermist. It's an art form, really; getting them so realistic and everything. That's what the paper said." Debbie smeared the coffee lipstick on her bottom lip and rubbed her lips together.

"I don't want to see them. I'll wait in the car." Riley folded his arms over his black T-shirt and buried his chin into the collar.

"What? Riley, we're here already. Come on. Your dad and I really thought you'd like this."

He stared at the bobbing compass on the dash. If Debbie thought a little begging would make him change his mind, she was wrong. But what if she told Dad he wasn't getting along with her? Then what would happen?

"Look. I guess I should have talked about this before we came here. But... Hey, you can pick the lunch spot. Just give it a try, okay?" Debbie begged.

Riley looked at her. She had a sad puppy kind of look on her face, mouth drooping, eyes drooping. She reminded him of Rufus—the dog she packed in the car, even though she didn't want to.

"Well, okay. But we won't be long, will we?" Riley checked the lizards before he got out of the car. They were on the sides of the glass cage, waiting for something. Their black eyes darted back and forth.

"Don't worry, guys. I'll keep her away from you."

3
Disgusted Lizards

Debbie closed the gopher museum door behind them. Black darkness surrounded Riley, as if he'd been caught and stuffed into a covered cage. He shuffled toward sparks of light coming from boxes mounted on the walls.

"Hello there!" a voice crackled. A woman with gray hair piled on top of her head stepped from a door at the back of the room. She studied Riley over the tops of her silver wire glasses. "There's a two-dollar admission charge," she said. Riley searched the room for Debbie.

"I'll take care of that." Debbie moved past him, digging in her purse. "You go ahead, Riley. I'll catch up in a minute."

The first scene was the Torrington Village Office. The walls were painted with trees and a building. Two dead gophers played tug of war with another dead gopher as the rope.

"This one is needed for the museum" was written on paper stuck above one gopher's head.

"Sick!" Riley mumbled so Debbie couldn't hear him.

Riley thought about leaving right away and waiting outside by the car. But what would Dad say if he found out? He heard Debbie's clicking heels behind him.

"So? Pretty neat, huh?" she said, peering into the case. "Ha! Did you see that?" Debbie pointed at the sign posted in front of the three gophers in the box. It read: G.A.G.S. (Gophers Against Getting Stuffed). Riley didn't think it was funny at all.

"You get it, Riley?" She pushed her elbow into his side. "It's a protest sign!"

Riley took a step back and rubbed where she'd poked him. He stared at the poor gopher in the middle. How could Debbie think this gopher museum was funny? What if someone decided to make a lizard museum in Florida where lots of lizards live?

"Yeah, I get it." Riley wandered to the back of the museum, away from the boxes. How long would it be until Debbie was finished?

"They're Richardson Ground Squirrels."

Riley nearly ran into the woman who had taken the admission. The old woman's flowery perfume was strong. It made the inside of Riley's nose tingle. "We call them gophers for the tourists," she said. "I bet you didn't know that."

"No." Riley tried to be polite. He wrapped his arms around himself; the room was much cooler than outside.

"There's over twenty-five of them here." The flowery lady touched Riley's arm and pointed to one of the boxes. "Did you see the one with the black fur? He's quite rare."

"No." Riley turned his back to her. His mom would never bring him to a place like this. He couldn't believe his dad would like it, either. Maybe Debbie was changing Dad.

"Hey, Riley." Debbie moved toward him. "Did you see this one of the Salt and Pepper Restaurant? One of the gophers at the table says, 'Oh boy, am I ever stuffed!' "

Riley rolled his eyes. He had to get out of here. He wondered how the lizards were doing. Maybe it was too hot; they could be burning up. Did they miss him? Were they lonely for him the way he was lonely for his mom, especially right now?

The museum lady started whispering to Debbie. Riley stared at the floor wishing they'd stop talking so he could leave.

"Riley. Florence has something she wants to show you. I told her how much you like science." Debbie smiled at the museum lady and nodded her head.

"The taxidermist gave us an extra gopher so we can show it to our patrons. I thought you'd like to see it." The old woman opened a door behind them and, before Riley could say no, she was back with a stiff gopher in her hand.

"Here." She held the animal out for him. "He's very light. He's got a core of Styrofoam in him."

"No, thanks." Riley stared at the animal. The old woman was stroking it as if it were alive. "I like holding real animals, not dead ones," he said. If he'd had any food in his stomach he might have actually vomited all over Florence, Debbie and the dead gopher.

"Oh," Florence answered. "I'm sorry. I thought you'd be interested." She hung her head down as she petted the gopher. Debbie's sharp fingernails glided over Riley's skin. She wrapped her fingers around his forearm. Riley gasped. He swallowed hard.

"I guess we'd better be going," Debbie snapped. She nudged Riley forward, her hand tightening around his arm. He didn't move.

"Do they die of old age? Or do you kill them?" His voice echoed in the quiet. Riley's stare met the old woman's eyes. She looked away.

"I guess there's no getting around it." The woman's bony hands shook. "The taxidermist traps them. On his own land, mind you. And then he puts them down." She cleared her throat. Riley waited for the whole story.

"Yes. He puts them to sleep. Then he stuffs them." She cleared her throat again. Riley stared at the dead gopher in the woman's hands. He felt sorry for him.

"It's noon," the woman said coldly. "We close at lunchtime you know. Thanks for coming." She turned her back to Riley and Debbie and busied herself moving paper around, waiting for them to go.

"Riley!" Debbie hissed. Her fingernails dug into Riley's arm. "Here's the key. Go get in the car. " She handed him her key ring. A picture of Dad and Debbie in a plastic frame was attached to it.

"Ow," he muttered, "you're hurting my arm." He glared at her. She stared back as if she wished he weren't there. Riley escaped.

He squinted at the sun pounding through his glasses all the way to the car. He wished he knew how to drive. If he did, he'd leave Debbie here and drive straight to Mom's house. Dad would probably understand. "Dad, it was torture," he'd say. "I had no choice." Riley stared at the picture. It would look much better if Debbie wasn't in it. He pushed the key in the door lock and turned it.

The plastic seat burned his legs. Lizzy and Megarra were still clinging to the sides of their cage. They weren't moving, even blinking. Frozen in fear, Riley thought. They knew what was inside that trailer; they read his mind.

Debbie stomped to her side of the car. She hit the window with her knuckles and pointed at the lock. Riley leaned over and pulled up the latch.

"That was so rude," she spit out after she had shut her door. "I had to apologize to her for how rude you were. Do you realize how you've embarrassed me? That poor woman was just being nice, telling you all that stuff and showing you the gopher. You know, this could have been a very educational side trip."

Debbie pulled the sunglasses from her purse and put them over her eyes. She backed out of the driveway so fast, Riley thought he was going to be sick. He watched the museum disappear at lightning speed.

He wished he could put his own sign on the outside of the car:

R.A.S.M.

(Riley Against Step Moms)

4
Angry Lizards

"The lizards need to eat, too," Riley said as they left the drive-through of the fast food place Debbie had picked. She hadn't kept her promise to let him decide. It must have been his punishment for being rude to the woman at the museum. How was wanting to know the truth about all those gopher deaths rude?

"I'm sure we can dig up something for them to eat. We've got tons of stuff in the cooler." Debbie placed a french fry in her mouth and smiled as she chewed.

"But lizards are insectivores. They eat insects like crickets. You have to buy them at the pet store." Riley watched Debbie's smile drop at the corners. He scratched the back of his neck, where the hair was starting to grow in from his last haircut.

Debbie's lips left a ring around the straw after she finished slurping. "I packed a fly swatter. While I'm setting up camp, you can kill some flies and feed them to the lizards—"

"Debbie—" Riley tried interrupting her but she talked too fast.

"—and we really have to work when we get there, Riley. I was counting on your help with the tent and the campfire. But, your lizards are important. So you can kill the flies instead. Then after…"

Riley ran his fingernail between his two front teeth, picking out the lettuce that was stuck there.

"Debbie?" Riley said it louder this time. She stopped talking and stared at him. She tucked her fluffy hair behind her ears.

"What is it, Riley?"

"The food has to be alive or the lizards won't eat it." Riley waited for Debbie to answer.

"What?"

Riley repeated himself.

"Why didn't you tell me this earlier? I had this day all planned out and…oh…never mind!" Debbie tapped her fingernail against the dash.

"I guess I just forgot." Maybe the lizards could go another couple of days, though. Riley couldn't exactly remember when he'd fed them last.

"For the record, I think it's revolting that those things have to eat live insects." Debbie poked her thumb toward Lizzy and Megarra. A massive logging truck thundered past them. The car leaned to the right. Riley held on tighter to the door handle.

"It's lizards this, lizards that. Why couldn't we just get to know each other better?" Debbie was almost yelling as she made the car go faster. All this over a few bugs? And she said she wanted to go camping?

"So, now you know what I felt like, having to go see dead gophers," Riley mumbled. He wasn't sure if Debbie heard him at first. Then he saw her clenching the steering wheel, her mouth shut tight. He turned back to his window. He saw the logging-truck driver's cigarette as they rocketed past him.

Debbie turned up the radio real loud. Riley closed his eyes and willed himself to sleep. At least if I'm not awake I won't be fighting with her.

He woke to Debbie's singing to the radio, still. Oh shut up, he thought. His neck hurt from the cramped position he'd been lying in. He'd pushed himself as far into the door as he possibly could, hoping he would just shrink to nothing and could escape the minute the car stopped.

The hot, spicy smell of burning campfires leaked into the car. They must be in the campground. Riley rolled down his window and scanned for campsite 42.

"Hey, there it is, on the right." A brown, weathered picnic table stood in a clearing off to the left. On the right, tall evergreen trees made a canopy over tangled bushes.

Debbie turned into the campsite and pulled off her glasses. Riley yanked on the door handle and swung the door open wide. He could probably figure out how to get to the playground, hiking trails, bathroom and activity center—all the important stuff—before dark.

"Wait a minute, Riley," Debbie said. "I want you to unpack the trunk while I deal with this bug problem. Then we'll set up the tent. I'm afraid there won't be any time for exploring tonight."

"Aww," Riley sighed, "no fair." He pulled out Debbie's bags and dropped them near the picnic table where Debbie sat. She had a hanger and a pair of pantyhose next to her.

"What are you doing?" Riley asked.

"Never mind. You've still got things to unpack. If you don't get moving, we'll be putting our tent up in the dark. You don't want to sleep on a pile of rocks, do you?" Riley shook his head. She waved her hands at him as if she were shooing away a fly.

Riley kicked the ground, sending the gravel flying on the way back to his chore. He was always doing what someone told him. He pulled the tent, camping gear, and sleeping bags from the trunk. At the very bottom, he found the ax.

The wood handle was dull at the end but shiny and worn down a bit where Dad held it when he was swinging. Riley removed the brown leather cover from the ax head. He always wanted to try chopping wood, but Dad said he was too young. Riley hefted the ax over his shoulder and took a few practice swings, slicing the air.

The sky had turned a deep blue. Calm, cerulean blue his mother called it, the color of the sea and the sky when all is peaceful. Maybe camping with Debbie would be okay once the lizards got fed.

He should get a fire started to help her. It was cooling down and they'd need one to make dinner. It couldn't be too hard to make a fire. He took the ax into the forest next to the campsite. There was a tree that was a bit taller than his dad and about five inches around with most of its branches at the top. He lifted the ax, taking careful aim at the trunk. He eyed the spot he wanted to hit and pulled the ax back over his head.

"Riley!"

His head jerked toward the noise. The ax flew out of his hands and landed in the bushes behind him.

It was Debbie, again! Why was she always ruining everything?

5
Chopping Lizards

"What are you doing with that ax?" Debbie stood at the edge of the trees. Probably everyone in the campground could hear her yelling. She stumbled through the bushes toward him.

"I was going to start a fire," he yelled back. He reached down to pick up the ax. He liked the feel of the smooth wood against his palms.

"Give me that thing!" Debbie snatched the ax from his hands. Her hair was littered with leaves and bits of twigs.

"You could have killed yourself with this. You don't cut down trees to start a fire. There's a huge stack of firewood next to the campsite." Her eyes were wide, and her cheeks were red. Her whole face looked like it might explode. She opened her mouth but closed it and turned her back to him. She took two steps forward and then faced him again.

"And another thing. I never said to play around with the ax, did I?" Debbie pointed her finger at him as she spoke, trying to pin the words on him. "I said unpack the trunk. Why can't you just do what I tell you?"

"Dad would let me do it if he was here. And so would my mom," Riley answered.

"But they're not here, are they?" she shouted back.

Riley stared at the ground. His eyes started to burn.

"Riley, I don't ever want to see you playing with this again," Debbie said, her voice shrinking. "Your mom and dad would want me to keep you alive. I know that."

Riley followed her through the trees. She stopped at the picnic table and faced him. He held his breath.

"Here's your bug catcher—go catch some bugs for those lizards." She held out a bent up coat hanger with a kind of net thing attached to it. Riley looked closer. It was her pantyhose. The hanger was bent into a circle with a handle on it, like the dippers he'd used to decorate Easter eggs with his mom last spring break. The top part that goes around the waist was sewn onto the hanger, making the underwear part the net. There were knots where the legs used to hang.

Riley folded his arms and stared right into Debbie's eyes.

"That's not going to work. The bugs will just fly out." Even if it did work, he didn't want to have anything to do with a pair of Debbie's pantyhose. Not even for the lizards.

"Actually, Riley, it does work. I already tried it when you were in the trees playing forest ranger." Debbie wasn't smiling at her joke. Riley could feel his face getting hot.

"All you have to do is swish the net right down in the bushes near the water over there." She pointed to the back of the clearing with a fingernail that was broken and jagged.

"Then you grab the net up near the waistband—I mean the edge there." She took the net from him to demonstrate. "When you get back to the cage, you lift the lid, put the net in, and let go of it. The bugs fly out and the lizards...Well, you know what the lizards do." Debbie shuddered like she had the creeps.

So Debbie had actually fed Lizzy and Meg. She must not have liked watching them eat. Riley thought it was cool how they stood absolutely still in the cage until something flew by and then they darted toward it, their jaws snapping shut fast as a lightning strike. With big crickets, the legs hung out the sides of Meg's mouth and disappeared with the second bite.

"Well?" Debbie shoved the sheer brown net toward him.

"I'll do it now," Riley mumbled. He knew Dad would be mad if Debbie told him about the ax. Maybe he could ask her not to tell him. No. She'd probably say no, anyway.

Riley made four trips from the bug hunting grounds to the lizard cage. Debbie was right, the net worked. In the meantime, she had laid the blue tent out flat and nailed in the outside stakes. She was now inside, putting up the middle pole. Riley thought he'd like to put the tent up, but he didn't want to bother Debbie. He checked on the lizards instead.

Lizzy was lying on the big rock in the middle of the cage—his eyes closed, his tail still. He looked a lot like Riley's dad on the couch after Thanksgiving dinner. Riley wondered if he'd let out a big belch. Meg was under the plant, her favorite spot. Riley stashed the net where he was sure no one would see it and joined Debbie at the firepit. Daylight had drifted away. The campsite was dark except for the lantern sitting on a wood stump near the wood-chopping block.

He was glad the day was almost over. There wasn't much time for him to mess anything else up.

"Riley, want to help me cut the kindling? The logs are too big to get the fire started so we've got to cut some small pieces. I'll show you how. I was a Girl Guide, you know." Riley noticed Debbie had changed clothes. She was wearing jeans and her blond hair was pulled back with a red bandana.

Stacks of wood in different sizes were piled in a semi-circle around the big wood block. The ax was driven into the center— Riley's Excalibur sword in the stone.

"Oh, I don't know." Riley shook his head.

"Aw, come on. If I can do it, so can you." Debbie's lips shone in the lantern light.

"Okay." He shrugged his shoulders. "I guess you'll make me do it anyway." Mosquitoes buzzed around his head.

"Great! Watch me once and then you can do it yourself." Debbie sat a log on the chopping block and checked to make sure it didn't wobble too much. She swung the ax. It got stuck near the edge of the log and she pounded the log onto the chopping block until she had sliced off a small piece of wood. Easy.

"There," she said. "Your turn." She drove the ax into the chopping block and moved back.

Riley stepped into her place, his hands sweating. It was easier out in the forest when she wasn't there to watch him. He wiped his hands on his jeans and pushed his glasses up his nose. He held the ax the way Debbie showed him, his hands spread apart. Then lifted the ax into the air, as far as his ears. His hands were wet again. The handle slipped a little. He gripped the ax tighter.

He grunted as he heaved his arms forward. The smack of the ax hitting wood answered. He almost hollered Yes! in victory. Then he saw the ax was stuck in the chopping block. He'd missed the log entirely! Riley's arms ached. It couldn't be that hard, could it? Debbie could do it.

"Good try, Riley. This time try looking at the log. Don't close your eyes. It's kind of like baseball. If you want to make contact, you've got to watch the ball."

Riley felt his face turning red. First she was a Girl Guide. What next? A pinch hitter for little league?

"I don't want to do it," he moaned. He didn't like it when he wasn't good at something the first time. Besides, he didn't want to chop kindling; he wanted to cut down a tree.

"What? Come on, Riley. It was just your first try. How are you going to learn if you give up?" Riley stared at the ax, still sticking in the block. Debbie kept right on talking.

"If I can do it, Riley, so can you." She sounded like she was training a puppy, telling it what a good dog it was when it peed in the grass. Riley didn't want to be her pet. Debbie pulled the bandana from her hair and wiped the ax handle. She lifted another log off the pile. This one was bigger.

"Debbie, I don't want to do this right now." Riley shoved his hands inside his pockets. He bit the inside of his lip.

"Here, Riley. This one will work better. I didn't pick out a very good log the first time around." Debbie held the ax out for him. Riley shook his head.

"I don't need you to make me feel better." Riley felt the place in the back of his throat get bigger and bigger and more achy and hot. "I don't need your stupid talking. Or your...your lipstick. I don't need any of this." His eyes burned. Debbie just stared at him. He felt stupid almost crying in front of her.

"I just want to go to my mom's house." He swallowed, drenching the fiery feeling. He felt the tears begin to stream down his face.

"I gotta go to the bathroom," he managed to squeak out as he ran away.

6
Hidden Lizards

Riley locked the door to the bathroom and ignored the people who knocked. Then a deep male voice said he was going to get the park ranger to open the door. Riley dried his glasses off and sneaked out after the footsteps had faded away.

"Hey, Riley." Debbie stood at the water pump near the bathrooms. "I'm sorry about everything."

Riley walked past her to the trail that led back to their campsite. He was glad it was dark so she couldn't see his face.

"I can see you don't want to talk about it tonight." He heard her sneakers rustling the pine needles on the trail behind him. "I was thinking we should wait until tomorrow, anyway. When we've calmed down a little."

Riley didn't answer. He walked even faster. The moon lit up the trail. He knew the stars would be shining. Dad had taught him how to find the Big Dipper and Orion, but he didn't want to look for them anymore.

When they got back to the campsite, the fire was gray ash with a few red spots. If he had been there with Dad, they'd be singing camp songs about Bill Grogan's goat and the cat that always came back. Mom would probably read scary ghost stories.

Instead of them, Riley was stuck with Debbie.

Riley shuffled into the tent and crawled into the green plaid sleeping bag with his clothes still on. He shoved his face into his Godzilla pillow when Debbie shone the flashlight into the tent. He heard the hushing of the zipper and Debbie's rustling. Finally, there was dull silence with a sighing breeze and buzzing insects.

"I brought the lizards in, their cage is near the door," Debbie whispered. "But we probably didn't even need to bother with the bug catcher. We could have just left the lid off the cage. There's enough bugs inside the tent for a hundred amphibians."

Riley didn't remind her that lizards are reptiles, not amphibians. He didn't check to see that Lizzy and Megarra were all right. He just wanted to sleep until the trip was over.

Debbie got up before Riley. He heard her moving around outside the tent, humming. He didn't recognize the song. It mingled with the clinking of pots and pans and the soft crunching of her footsteps near the campfire. It reminded him of his mom.

On Saturday mornings during the summer, she always brought him breakfast in bed. It was one of his favorite things about her. Mom would tiptoe through the kitchen, collecting a buffet of food. There would be a donut, pancakes, bacon, syrup, apple wedges, juice and sometimes a little bowl of Smarties for dessert.

They would sit on the bed and talk about what to do that day. She always let him pick. This summer there would only be three Saturdays. That just wasn't enough. Riley felt his throat ache in the very back. It was as dry as the desert. He remembered the lizards.

He opened his eyes and looked around. Rufus sat in-between Riley and Debbie's pillows. The lizard cage was at his feet, near the tent flaps that were lashed tight against the morning sun. Lizzy and Meg looked as dry as his throat felt. Riley fished their water spray bottle out of his bag and squirted the insides of the glass terrarium. It wasn't exactly like living in the wild, collecting water drops that cling to plant leaves. But, it worked.

Lizzy stretched across the wall, his tongue flicking out against the glass. Megarra lay on the rock. She didn't seem to want to drink. Maybe she was tired of being away from home. Riley opened the flap of the tent to give the lizards some sun.

"Breakfast is on," Debbie called. She didn't sound happy, but she didn't sound mad either.

"Okay," Riley groaned. He thought about curling back up in his sleeping bag for the rest of the day. He could tell Debbie he was sick. Maybe she would bring in his meals. Or maybe she would make him go to a doctor who would find nothing was wrong. He decided to get dressed.

The bright sun bounced off Riley's glasses. He raised his hand to shield his eyes. Couldn't it rain or something? His mouth felt like it was coated in gunk. He slid his tongue over his teeth.

"I made my specialty." Debbie was in the same sweatshirt and jeans as last night. She was already wearing her sunglasses. "Tex-Mex eggs." She put the cast-iron frying pan in front of him. Riley leaned over the steaming eggs.

"Be careful, the pan's hot," she warned quickly. She sounded like their neighbor who was always freaking out about her kid looking both ways before he crossed the road.

He pushed the fork through the eggs, red peppers and salsa all mixed together. This was his favorite breakfast, his and Dad's. Riley ate slowly. The hot salsa made his eyes water and his nose run. He couldn't imagine there was any more liquid left in him.

"Riley." Debbie set a glass of orange juice in front of him. "I know I talk a lot and maybe you don't really want to listen to me at all. But I just want you to know that it's okay if you don't feel like camping." Debbie ran her fingers through her hair, pulling it back and then fluffing it out.

The mosquito bites on Riley's back and arms and scalp itched. He stared at a big red one on his elbow and ran his short, dirt-filled fingernails over it.

"I phoned your mom this morning. I managed to get her on her cell phone. She's on some shoot north of Vancouver—Port Hardy I think she said."

Riley scratched harder. Debbie called Mom? Oh, man. She'd probably be mad.

"I told her you were getting tired of camping and you'd like to come to Vancouver early." Debbie's perfume mixed in with the smell of campfire smoke.

"She made a phone call then phoned me back," Debbie continued. "She said you can come today if you want. Her boyfriend Keene will take a few days off and stay with you at the apartment until she gets back."

Riley swallowed his juice down in one gulp. He could go to Vancouver today, but he would have to stay with Keene? He hardly knew Keene. Mom had the guy over for dinner twice during spring break. Why couldn't Mom finish up early to be with him? Now he had to choose Keene or Debbie?

7

Confused Lizards

"**S**o, it's up to you now, buddy." Debbie punched him lightly on the arm. "What'll it be? Another night in bugville, or a comfy bed?"

Riley scratched harder. He noticed a bite on his knee, too. He rested his foot on the picnic bench and stared at the red mark.

"Vancouver." He scratched some more. Debbie shuffled her plate, fork, knife and cup on the table.

"I know you miss your mother, Riley. It's okay if you don't want to be with me." Her voice wavered like a note on a piano after you hit one of the keys. Riley was afraid she was going to cry. He didn't want to see that.

"I still think you're a terrific kid." The fire spat and crackled. Campers from nearby campsites crunched in the gravel road toward the trails. Debbie shifted next to him and then left the table.

"I think we better get moving if we're going to make Vancouver tonight." She dumped all the dirty dishes into the cardboard box next to him. She was trying to be cheerful, but Riley could tell she was faking it.

He grabbed his backpack from the tent and walked the trail to the bathroom. He saw the playground off to his right. He had wanted to try out the zip line. He could see a bunch of kids waiting for their turn. Maybe next time, he thought. Maybe Dad would bring him here next summer. As long as someone else didn't die. And if he wasn't still mad about this trip with Debbie.

Riley squeezed the green paste onto his toothbrush. It wasn't really his fault, was it? Debbie was the one who called. Not him. He probably would have been fine going hiking like they planned and then fishing tomorrow. He spit the foam into the sink.

Fishing.

He'd forgotten that if they were going to Vancouver today, he wouldn't be fishing tomorrow in Kamloops. And that was going to be the best part of the drive to Vancouver. Dad had set it up. Dad's friend Dan had a fishing lodge on Badger Lake. That's where he was going to learn how to fish. That's where he was going to catch Big Stella. The big one that got away, Dad had told him.

Riley threw his backpack over his shoulder and headed to the campsite. Maybe he could tell Debbie he didn't want to stay with Keene after all. He ran the rest of the way to the campsite.

Debbie already had the tent packed into the trunk of the car. The cardboard box of dishes was in there, too. Riley saw his lizard cage in the back seat next to Rufus and his Godzilla pillow. She wouldn't want to unpack now. He stared at his sneakers, brown covered from the dusty trail.

"Hey, Riley." Debbie sounded cheerful. "Give me ten more minutes and we're outta here!" She thumbed toward the highway. "I called my girlfriend, Amy, and she's all set for me to come a couple days early." She slid the ax in the trunk alongside the tent.

"You know, I think it'll work out fine if we go now," she added. "This way you'll be settled for your mom and be in your room for a couple of extra days."

When Debbie finished loading their stuff, Riley got in the car, buckled his seat belt and peered into the lizard cage.

Megarra was sitting on the sunning rock; her skin was brown and it clung tight to her ribs. He could see them moving in and out with every breath. She was under stress.

Shouldn't I be happy the trip is almost over? Riley tried to transmit the message though brainwaves.

Megarra blinked.

Did she understand how he felt? He wanted someone to tell him he made the right choice.

She blinked again.

Maybe she felt as confused as he did.

Riley closed his eyes as they were backing up. He didn't want to see the campsite disappearing. He was tired of saying goodbye. He listened to the radio and eventually fell asleep hoping Keene had stopped smoking cigars by the time they got to Vancouver.

"Are you getting hungry?" Debbie pulled off the highway at a big sign that read REVELSTOKE—DOWNTOWN. "You must be really tired, Riley; you haven't done anything but sleep for the past three hours."

"Mmm," Riley groaned. The sun blared through the windshield, right into his eyes. He pulled his Edmonton Trappers baseball cap out of his backpack and stuck it on his head. They passed a red train engine with an endless chain of coal cars behind it. A man in the engine waved when he saw Debbie waving at him.

"That's what I like about these small towns," Debbie said. "The people are so friendly. Isn't it beautiful, Riley?"

Riley saw more mountains, more trees and more boring little houses.

"They put tin roofs on the buildings here." Debbie pointed toward Riley's side of the street. "It's because of all the snowfall they get. The snow just slides right off the roofs. You see what I'm talking about, Riley?" She leaned over. Her hair touched his shoulder.

"Yeah, I see it," Riley muttered. Why couldn't they just go somewhere? Why was she always trying to teach him something? First the gophers, then the wood chopping, now the roofs. He looked out the front window. He saw red brake lights on the car ahead of them.

"Debbie! Watch out!" Riley felt the car's brakes being slammed on. But it was too late. Smash! He saw it all like he was seeing a movie. Debbie's car crashed and bounced off the gold-painted car in front of them. Riley's chest hit, thwack, against the seatbelt and for a second he couldn't breathe. The screech and scrape sounds echoed one after the other. Then silence. Fast, raspy breaths were squeezed into the quiet.

Riley noticed Debbie's sunglasses were hanging in two parts from her ears. The middle section must have broken when her face hit the steering wheel. He saw a red mark between her eyes.

"Debbie," Riley said. "Your glasses." Riley reached up to check his own glasses. They were still together.

"Oh!" Debbie grunted. The two halves shook as she examined them. "I guess I should have a car with airbags," she mumbled. Debbie squinted out the front window into the sunshine. She took two deep breaths.

The driver got out of the car they'd hit. He was short and covered in gold that shimmered, gold rings, a gold watch, and gold chains around his neck. He was like King Midas in the fairytale—

everything he touched turned to gold. The man ran his hand along his gold car, patting it to make sure it was all right.

"It figures I'd hit a BMW," Debbie whispered as she swung her door open. Clunk. She closed the door behind her and stood next to the man.

The man pulled out his cell phone and jammed his finger into the numbers. He cursed.

Debbie stood with her hands on her hips. Her mouth was moving fast. Riley heard a few words. "We're on our way to Vancouver…promised him we'd be there tonight…deal with this later…doesn't seem to be any damage."

The man's neck was turning red as Debbie talked. He shuffled his feet and punched more numbers into the phone. He marched back to the door of his car and threw the phone in through the open window.

"Would you just shut up!" he yelled. He ran his hand through his golden wave of hair. The redness was creeping up his face.

"Ow." Riley winced like the man had yelled at *him*. The man seemed seriously mad, too mad. Riley locked his door and curled up on the seat, his knees at his chest with his arms wrapped around them.

8

Courageous Lizards

Midas stepped toward Debbie. She backed up to her door. Riley could see her face now. It was pale with red splotches. She must be scared. Riley uncurled himself. He had to do something. But what?

He could see that the train engineer Debbie had waved to earlier stood next to the tracks. He was looking in their direction. Why wouldn't he come over to help?

"I think we should take a few minutes to calm down," Debbie said as her hand reached for the door handle. The man grabbed her wrist.

"Let go of me." Debbie yanked her arm back. Thud. Her fist hit the car window. The man moved closer.

"Do you realize what you've done?" The man pointed his finger at her and poked at the middle of her chest. Debbie's shoulders lifted and her body jerked back each time his finger hit her. "That is a brand-new BMW." The man's lips pulled back like a fierce dog, his teeth flashed. Riley could see the veins in his neck popping out.

"I bought it yesterday in Vancouver. I was just out for a drive." He sounded like he had pebbles in the back of his throat. His hand moved up to Debbie's shoulder.

"Look, just calm down. I'll pay for it. Whatever the damage is. Just let me go," Debbie pleaded. Riley had to do something.

"I don't want any money. I have lots of money. I want my BMW the way it was." The angry face was only inches from Debbie's. Riley could see the spit pooling on the man's bottom lip.

Riley threw open his door and jumped out.

"Help! Help! Call 911! We need help!" he screamed.

"Riley, get back in the car," Debbie hissed. Riley shook his head. He wasn't moving until that man left Debbie alone. The train engineer ran across the street toward them.

"Hey, buddy." The train engineer stood behind the rich guy. "Let go of her." He was nearly a head taller than Midas and big like a wrestler.

"This is none of your business." The angry man shot a look at the engineer but his eyes turned back to Debbie. Debbie reached up and wiped at the red spot he'd left on her chest.

"Back off," she snarled. "You're scaring my little boy."

"You heard her," Riley yelled. He knew Midas couldn't hurt him with the train engineer there. "Back off." His whole body was shaking.

The engineer grabbed the rich guy's arm.

"Leave me alone," Midas yelled. "She's the idiot who dented my car." He pulled his arm back and nearly put an elbow into the train driver's chest.

"It's just a bumper," Debbie said. "I said I'd pay for it."

"That's not good enough." Midas stayed put. Passing cars were slowing down, the drivers looking to see what was going on.

Riley moved to the front of their car. The BMW's shiny silver bumper had a dent about the size of a football, and Debbie's car was pushed in a little at the front and the headlight was broken.

"Whatever the damage is, I'm sure the police will tow it to the garage for you while they book you for assault," the engineer said as he stepped closer to Midas and pulled him away from Debbie.

"Assault? What are you talking about?" Midas shrugged his shoulders.

"You can't hurt people. It's against the law," Debbie answered.

"Yeah!" Riley stared at the man.

"I need to phone my lawyer!" Midas growled as he stalked back to his car. He slammed the door behind him. Screech! Riley held his hand over his ears at the squealing of the tires against the pavement.

"Hey! He's getting away." Riley noticed two black streaks on the street where the car had been.

"Figures. I've got his license number, though," Debbie said. "We just have to give it to the police."

"Are you okay?" the train engineer asked Debbie. "I'm sorry I didn't come sooner. I didn't realize what was going on till your son yelled for help."

"Yeah, I'm okay." Debbie shook her head and laughed. "And I just finished telling Riley about all the friendly people here." Her laugh didn't sound normal at all.

"How about you?" the engineer asked Riley. "Are you okay? That's pretty scary watching your mom get treated like that, isn't it?"

"Yeah, really scary." Riley was going to tell him she was his stepmom but it just didn't seem that important right now. Riley wiped his nose with the bottom of his T-shirt. "Can we go now?"

41

9
Green Lizards

"This must be the place." Debbie stopped in a clearing at the end of the dirt road. She'd picked up dinner to go so they could have a picnic. Riley had agreed, hoping the BMW driver would be far ahead of them when they started driving again.

Speckles of light fell on the sign—BEGBIE FALLS. Riley looked up at the long pine tree branches that made a roof over his head. The lizards were lying lazily on the bottom of the cage, cool at last. He got out and stretched; his body had become a wobbly rubber band.

"Can you hear the waterfall, Riley?" Debbie called back to him from the trail head. Riley listened. The water sound rushed through his ears. He'd never seen a waterfall. He tucked in his shirt and followed Debbie down the trail. She had the backpack with the sandwiches in it. It was the same chocolate color as her fingernails.

"It's a little steep but manageable," Debbie cautioned.

Riley's sneakers slipped on the moss-covered ground. Pine cones crunched under his feet.

"I'm sorry for what happened," Debbie yelled. She hugged a tree and stepped down at the same time.

Riley concentrated on the trail. His sneakers thudded on the wooden posts staked into the ground for steps.

"That accident was my fault," Debbie continued. "I should have paid more attention to the road. I was trying so hard to make the trip interesting or fun or...I don't know. I guess I just screwed it all up." She stood at the bottom of the hill, her hands on her hips. She looked so small.

Riley picked his way through big tree roots. His feet slid under him. "Ow!" He landed on his rear. Something sharp stabbed the palm of his hand. It was a strange looking pine cone; all the spikes were glued together. He put it in his pocket and sprinted the last few steps. He skidded to a stop next to Debbie.

"It was just an accident," Riley said. He gripped the pine cone in his pocket. "It wasn't your fault."

"You really think so?" Debbie had taken her sunglasses off. Riley hadn't noticed before that her eyes were green.

"Yeah," said Riley. "But what a jerk to run into." He kicked the ground, sending stray pine cones flying.

"You're right about that." Debbie rubbed the spot on her chest. "But he won't get away with it. Not with my report and the engineer's and your testimony, too."

Riley nodded. The policeman at the station had explained that with so many witnesses, once they arrested the man he would probably plead guilty. Riley could feel his face getting hot again just thinking about that guy.

"Here we are in the middle of a beautiful forest, let's talk about something else." Debbie wiped away the tears that had fallen down her cheeks.

"Look at this." Riley gave Debbie the pine cone from his pocket. "I didn't recognize it at first, but I think it's a Jack pine cone. They only open up after a forest fire. The heat of the fire melts the resin that holds the cone together. When it bursts open, seeds are released. Then the seeds start rebuilding the forest. We learned about it during our forestry unit this year."

"Cool." Debbie's fingers touched Riley's as she gave the cone back.

Riley made a fist around the pine cone and squeezed tight. The jagged edges cut into his palm. "What was wrong with that guy? Was he crazy?"

"Mentally ill? I guess he might have been. Maybe he just has a short fuse." Debbie dropped the backpack from her shoulders.

"What do you mean, short fuse?"

"Well, he keeps all the things that bother him inside and then when something happens that makes him mad, his anger blows up like a bomb." Debbie squeezed her water bottle at her mouth. Water splashed across her face. She dried it off with the back of her hand.

Riley shuffled his feet in the pine-needle-covered ground. He remembered his phone conversation with Mom about summer holidays. When she'd told him he could only come for three weeks, he'd said, "That's okay. I know you're busy," and "I love you, too," before he hung up the phone. Then he'd run to his room, slammed his door and whispered into his pillow so even the air couldn't hear. "I hate you!" He had felt ready to explode, hadn't he?

Riley's head hurt. He was glad Debbie was zipping up the backpack and didn't notice he was almost crying.

"I'll meet you at the falls." Riley ran down the trail that wound along the riverbank and stopped at a wooden platform. Water poured over a cliff in front of him. Blood pounded in his ears and mixed with the sound of rushing water. A fine water mist sprayed Riley's face.

Riley heard Debbie breathing hard next to him. He took off his glasses and wiped them with the bottom of his T-shirt.

"Wow, isn't this magnificent?"

"Magnificent."

The platform was small. Debbie stood so close he could smell her perfume. If he wanted to, he could hold her hand or touch her arm. He crossed his arms over his chest.

"You know, Riley, we'd better have our lunch and get back on the road if we're going to make it to Vancouver tonight. We're still six hours away and it's after one p.m."

Vancouver. Keene. Cigars and empty beer bottles. Riley dug the Jack pine cone out of his pocket and threw it as far as he could. It hit a tree trunk and bounced into the waterfall.

"Good throw." Debbie smiled.

"Debbie, I want to go fishing," Riley blurted out.

"Now?" Debbie asked. "I don't think there are many fish here, Riley. And we don't have any fishing gear."

"No, not here. At Dan's fishing camp."

"You mean tonight?" Debbie asked. Riley nodded his head.

"Well, we can go if you want to. But if you're worried about running into that jerk, I promise I'll get you to your mom's safely." Debbie scratched a mosquito bite on her arm.

"It's not that. I just want to go fishing." Riley said. If Mom wasn't going to be home anyway, why get there just to wait for her?

 **10**

Fishing Lizards

Debbie stopped the car at the heavy metal chain that blocked the dirt road. She honked the horn. Cars weren't allowed right in the camp so they'd have to carry their gear down.

A figure crashed through the forest towards them. It had to be Dan, he had a vest with fishing lures hanging out of every pocket.

"Hey, Riley. How's your old man?" Dan held out his hand. Riley grabbed it and squeezed, the way Dad had taught him.

"Fine," Riley said. He'd never thought of Dad as an old man. "He wanted to come," Riley added.

"Yeah," Dan nodded his head. "It's been a long time. Hey, you must be Debbie." Dan pulled the bag from her arms. "I'll carry this," he said.

"Riley, grab your gear and head down to Cabin 5. You got your own place tonight," Dan said.

Riley's knees knocked the bottom of the lizard cage as he stumbled through the poplar and lodge pole pine trees that guarded the lake. He saw small cabins staggered along the lakeshore and in the middle of them was a bigger cabin—almost a house but not quite.

A large, yellow dog lay on the mat in front of Cabin 5's doorway. Riley started whistling, hoping to wake him up. It didn't work. Dan wouldn't have a dog that would bite a customer, would he? Still... Riley leaned over to look at the dog's face. His eyes were closed, the nose was dark brown and wet, the ears lay like a carpet over the top of his head.

"Hey, buddy," Riley whispered. "It's me, Riley. Don't bite. Okay?" The dog stood up, shook himself and walked away. Smart dog!

Riley set the lizard cage down where the dog had been. The lizards were jumping around like crazy. It must have been because of all the bugs in the air. Or maybe they had some instinct that told them this was the wilderness, like where they came from. Riley opened the door to Cabin 5.

Two wooden bunks stuck out from the wall with a curtain hung between them. A small window looked out onto the lake. On one wall there was a bar with hangers on it and metal hooks. Nothing spectacular. Not even a TV to watch scary movies after Debbie went to bed.

Then Riley saw a fish with silver, pinky-red and green-blue scales nailed on the wall. The tail fanned up and out as if it had frozen the instant it leaped out of the water. Under the fish was a small gold label. RAINBOW TROUT—KIP'S DREAM. Kip? That was Riley's dad's name. Did Dad catch that fish? Riley heard a knock on the door and then a squeak as it opened.

"Debbie said you'd want this." Dan set Rufus down. The stuffed dog fell over, his red tongue dragging on the wood floor.

"Oh, yeah. Thanks." Riley felt his face turning red. Dan probably thought it was silly to bring a stuffed dog on a fishing trip. But he didn't seem to care. He took his hat off and then put it back on, pulling the brim down tight. His curly hair fuzzed up around the edges.

"I see you've spotted your dad's legacy, have you?" Dan smiled wide. "He's a fine fisherman, your dad."

"That's not Big Stella, is it? Riley asked. "Dad said she was waiting here for me."

"No. Big Stella's still out in the drink." Dan's icy blue eyes sparkled, the lines at the corners turned up in a smile. "He caught that one before you were even a twinkle in his eye. He let me keep it here. I guess it wasn't gonna match the fancy decorating of your mom and dad's house."

Debbie knocked at the door. "Hey, are you guys ready to go fishing?"

"Yes, ma'am. We're just coming now." Dan hooked his thumbs through his belt loops. "You ready, Riley?"

Riley didn't answer. He was too busy thinking. Dan knew his mom. He knew her when she was still married to Dad.

"Riley?" Dan's eyes were kind.

He would probably talk to Riley about her, too.

"Yeah?" Riley said. They would have to talk when Debbie wasn't around.

"Are you ready to go?" Dan scratched the beard hairs on his face.

"Sure." Riley pulled his hat off and put it back on, pulling the brim right above his eyes. He followed Dan out the door.

"I put the best fly in my tackle box on your line," Dan told Riley as they got settled into the canoe.

Riley's hands sweated. He gripped his rod tighter. Maybe he couldn't chop wood but he could catch a fish, he told himself.

Riley was at the front of the canoe but turned around backwards. He watched Dan knot the end of Debbie's line around a single hook with fuzzy brown strings on it. It was supposed to look like a mosquito.

"It's finally cooling down around here, the fish will be feeding up a storm." Dan's paddle slipped into the water—slurp, clop. "Now let the line out a little at a time as we move forward in the water. The line you got there is a wet line. It'll sink down just a bit to where the fish are feeding."

Riley let out the fishing line as they traveled along the shore. He ran his tongue over his lips. They were starting to get chapped. He'd better not tell Debbie, she might try putting chocolate lipstick on him. He wondered if the lizards were getting hot, too.

The sun blasted him in the face when he faced forward in the canoe. He pulled his hat off and put it back on, pulling the brim right above his eyes. He was ready for a fish, he knew one was coming any second. It had to.

 **11**

Catching Lizards

"**S**he's catching flies, Riley," Dan's low voice hummed in the lake noises of buzzing insects and water slapping against the canoe.

Riley turned his head to see what Dan was talking about. Debbie's head rested on an extra life jacket and a slight snoring noise cut through the air.

"Yeah, rough day," Riley said. He scanned across the lake, happy there weren't any BMWs around.

"Ooh! Ooh!" Debbie yelled. The canoe shook underneath him. Riley jerked his head around.

"What is it?" he said.

"Looks like she's got a bite," Dan answered. Debbie was sitting up now. She grabbed the rod before it jumped out of the boat. The line was trailing out of the reel fast, too fast. Shouldn't she be pulling the fish in? If Dad were here he'd know what to do.

"What are you doing? He's going to take the rod with him," Riley yelled.

"Relax there, Riley. She knows what she's doing. She's setting the hook in the mouth. Then she'll reel her in." Dan was still paddling.

Relax? Debbie was on her knees now. One leg was braced against the side of the canoe. She pulled the rod back like she was going to chop wood. The tip of the rod was almost bent all the way over. She turned the reel a few times.

"She's a fighter," Debbie groaned.

"Is it a big one?" Riley yelled at Dan.

"I'd say it's a big one all right. I haven't seen one fight like that in a long time. Riley, reel your line in so it doesn't get tangled with Debbie's. We'll put it out again after we get this baby in the boat."

"Is it Big Stella, Dan?" Riley wasn't sure he wanted to know, but he had to ask.

"Sure could be."

Riley's line drifted with the waves as he reeled it in. His first time out fishing and with the best fly, too. Why couldn't it be him with Big Stella on the line?

Debbie pulled back on her rod, reeled in a few more times and then let a little bit out. Back and forth, back and forth. It was going to take all night for her to get the fish in. There wouldn't be time left for any more fishing.

"Riley, once you get that line in, you can grab the net. We'll need you to scoop her up," Dan said.

Riley turned the handle even faster. Yank! The rod flew forward. He grabbed it before it landed in the lake. "Dan!" he yelled. "Something's wrong with my rod." Riley kept pulling on the handle, trying to turn it back. His hand slipped. The line started trailing out again.

"Whoa," Dan hollered. "Looks like we got two on the line. Good going, Riley. Let the line out to set the hook. What a fast learner."

Riley didn't stop to tell Dan that it was just an accident; he never meant for the line to go out. He concentrated on reeling and letting go.

"Good job, Riley," Dan shouted. "Keep him tied up. We want to wear him out so he doesn't let go before we get him in the boat."

Maybe Dan was wrong and Debbie didn't have Big Stella. Maybe she was on Riley's line. He imagined his fish hanging in his bedroom, right above his bed. Dad would be so excited. Maybe Mom would paint a picture of him holding it. Riley's hat was slipping down. He pulled it off and shoved it into the canoe. Then his fish made a run for it. The fish crossed from the left side of the canoe over to the right.

Riley grabbed on to the rod with both hands and pulled it toward his shoulders. The line snapped. Riley jerked back. He dropped into the bottom of the canoe. His rod clattered next to him. The canoe rocked to the left and then the other way, right into the water. A splash came in, soaking his hat.

"Whoa!" Riley said.

"Hang on!" Dan shouted.

Riley held onto the gunnels with both hands to keep from falling out of the canoe.

"Oh no!" Debbie yelled. Riley heard a splash. Debbie was in the lake. Her rod was still in the canoe, the line running out fast.

"Riley. Take my rod. She's still on there," Debbie bubbled through the water. Riley grabbed the rod and started reeling in the slack.

"Are you okay, Debbie?" he asked. Debbie's fluffy hair was stuck to her head in wet clumps.

"Yeah, yeah, yeah," Debbie laughed. "Just get that fish in for me, will you?" Debbie swam for the nearby shore.

"I don't know if I can." Riley's hands shook. What if it really was Big Stella?

Riley yanked and reeled for what seemed like an hour. His arms ached even more than when he had tried chopping wood. His fingers burned from holding the rod so tight.

"Okay, Riley, hold her steady." Dan moved forward in the canoe with the net. "Just a bit more. As soon as we see her color, I'll slide my net under her."

Riley's hands slipped on the rod. His fingers tightened around the handle again. The mosquito bite on the back of his neck itched.

"There she is," Dan whispered.

Riley saw silver lightning under the water. Dan moved quickly. There was a small splash as the net went into the water and then the canoe rocked back. Dan set the fish into the canoe.

"Look at her!" Dan yelled. "What a beauty you caught there Riley. She must be fifteen pounds." A fat, silver fish with rainbow streaks all over her belly flopped at Riley's feet.

"Is it Big Stella?"

"Hey, if it ain't Big Stella it must be her mother." Dan clapped Riley on the back.

"Debbie!" Riley screamed across the lake. "I caught her! I mean, we caught her! Big Stella."

Riley saw her giving the thumbs up sign. "Good job!" Her voice drifted over the water.

"Now what do we do, Dan?" Riley took his hat off and put it on backwards. He peered at the fish gills moving in and out.

Dan held a baseball bat the size of a telephone in his hand.

"We just knock her on the head with the fish bonker, and then we can take her and get her stuffed."

"You mean you're going to kill her?" Riley asked.

"That's what you have to do to stuff em, Riley." Dan smiled. "Or we could let her go. I'd just have to pull the hook out of her mouth."

Riley imagined the bedroom wall again, the painting his mother would give him. Then he thought about the gophers and Lizzy and Megarra. He stared at Big Stella. He could see her eye staring up at him. He wondered if she knew what was coming next.

Riley looked over at the shore. He thought about yelling out, asking Debbie what she thought, but she was too far away. He'd just have to decide on his own. "I think we should let her go," he said.

"The customer is always right." Dan held the fish in one hand and eased the hook out of her mouth. Riley helped lift her from the canoe and slide her back into the lake. He leaned over the edge of the canoe and watched Stella disappear in the brown-gray water. He breathed deep. Everything was okay again.

"We've got another half-hour before dark," Dan's voice broke the silence. "Do you want to fish some more or would you like to go back in? Or…wait, I've got an idea. Do you want to see where your parents got married?"

"My mom and dad got married here?" Riley asked.

"Right over there." Dan pointed to the island at the far end of the lake.

"Yeah, I'd like to see that," Riley said.

12
Lost Lizards

It was dark when they got back to the fishing lodge. Riley passed tree branches strewn with Debbie's wet clothes as they hiked from the dock to the campfire. Dan went into the big cabin to make dinner. Riley headed to his cabin to change. The yellow dog nudged his hand with his nose.

"You want to come in?" Riley shoved the door open. The dog pushed past him bringing the smells of fishy lake water and campfire smoke with him. Riley turned on the light switch. A single lamp on the dresser cast Riley's shadow against the wall. He pulled off his jeans and his sweatshirt and threw them on the bed closest to the door. The dog jumped on top of them. A spray of dirt clods showered the floor.

"Hey! I don't think you're supposed to be up there," Riley said. The dog's eyes begged Riley to let him stay on the bed. "Okay. But just for a little while. I don't want you to get me in trouble."

The lizard cage sat on the chair next to the bed. Debbie must have brought them inside. The lizards were resting on the sandy bottom. He pulled the lid off and scooped Lizzy out. The lizard poked his head through the hole Riley made with his hands. Riley sat on the edge of the bed and held his face in front of Lizzy's.

"Hey, bud. I caught the biggest fish in the lake. Big Stella. But you'd be proud of me. I let her go. Just for you. And for her, too." Riley stroked Lizzy's back. The lizard turned grass green.

Riley could feel dog breath on his shoulder. Then a wet tongue on his neck and ear. "Cut it out," Riley giggled. He stood up and set Lizzy back in the cage.

"You guys are probably thirsty," he said. Riley pulled his bag off the hook in the back of the cabin. He put on a clean pair of sweatpants and grabbed the water bottle. He squirted water until it rained on the plant and the sides of the lizard cage. Riley waited for Lizzy and Megarra to come out to drink. He couldn't see them. He moved the plant around, lifted the rock. They weren't there.

Where had they gone? The lid was next to the chair where he'd left it. The lizards couldn't have climbed out that fast, could they? He'd left the lid off tons of times and they'd never gotten out, never in four years. It didn't make sense.

Unless.

Riley saw the dog at the head of the bed staring down into the corner, his tail swinging back and forth, his tongue dripping slobber onto the green plaid pillowcase.

"Dog! Get out!" Riley pulled at the dog's collar. He jumped off the bed and stared up at Riley like he was waiting for a treat.

"Get out!" Riley screamed again. He opened the door to the cabin.

"Get out!" He pushed the dog toward the door as hard as he could. The dog ran away, his tail wagging. Riley slammed the door behind him.

Riley scrambled over the bed and looked down at the corner where the two walls met. He thought he could see a lizard down there. He reached his hand down.

"Riley! What's the matter? Why are you screaming?" Debbie brought a rush of cool air into the cabin.

"Shut the door," Riley ordered.

"Riley, answer me," Debbie said, "What is going on?"

"The lizards are loose. I've got to catch them."

"I'll help," Debbie said.

"No. I'm supposed to take care of them."

"What?" Debbie sighed. She crossed her arms and leaned against the door.

Riley crawled on his stomach under the bed. A lizard ran past him, into the space between the log wall and the floor. He grabbed Lizzy before he could dart the other way. He dropped him into the cage and put the lid on.

"You got one." Debbie said. "Now can I help you look for the other one?'

"You can do what you want," Riley said. "But Megarra might not even be alive. Maybe the dog ate her."

"Dogs don't eat lizards, Riley."

Riley stared at her. What did she know?

"Okay, so I don't know what lizards eat, but I do know that dogs eat dog food. Have you ever met a dog that eats lizards?"

Riley ignored her. He got down on his hands and knees. He could hardly see his own hands in the dark and dusty edges of the cabin. How was he ever going to find Megarra?

"Let's look behind this dresser," Debbie suggested. "I'll pull it out, you look." Debbie pulled one end an inch away from the wall.

Riley's glasses scratched the wall as he peered down the black crack. The darkness flickered; it could be Meg's tail. "I think that's her. You have to pull the dresser out on your side, and then scare her so she'll come to me."

Debbie shoved her fingers between the dresser and the wall and pulled. The lizard moved.

"Quick! She's closer to you. Scare her!"

Debbie bent down and shook her hands at the floor. "Shoo," she said. The lizard darted toward Riley. His hands reached to clamp down on her body. Then Meg changed direction.

"She's coming toward you. Grab her!" Riley shouted.

Debbie crouched down, her hands open. "No. I don't want to touch it." She squealed and looked the other way. "Hey, I've got it. I did it!" She lifted her hands to her chest and stood up.

Riley's hands wrapped around a lizard body at the same time. He stood up smiling. His hands cupped around Meg, her head rested between his thumb and first finger. "No," he said. "I've got her."

"Then what's this?" Debbie's hand opened. A lizard tail twitched furiously, making a dozen *s* shapes. "Ahh!" she screamed.

 **Talking Lizards**

Debbie threw the wiggling tail on the ground. It was still moving like a kite in a windstorm.

"Oh no!" Riley opened his hand. Megarra was still in his palm but without her tail. His stomach felt sick. "She lost her tail."

"Lost her tail?" Debbie held her hands over her mouth and nose, breathing deep. "It looks like it got cut off and it's still alive." She moved toward the bed, stepping around the shaking tail.

Riley stroked Meg's back. Her skin was brown with green splotches. Did it hurt to lose a tail? Was Megarra mad that he hadn't kept her safe?

"Debbie, what should we do with the lizard tail?" Riley asked.

"Oh, Riley. I am so sorry." Debbie held her hand over her chest. "I suppose we could bury her. Along with her tail by the creek." Debbie sighed. "And I thought this trip couldn't get any worse."

Riley was confused. "Bury Meg? Why should we bury her? She's not dead."

"Well, I mean when she dies. I don't know how long it will take, do you?" Debbie twisted a strand of hair around her finger, dropped it and grabbed another piece to twist.

"They can live about eight years and she's four now." Meg began to climb up Riley's arm, her feet tickling his skin.

"But Riley, the lizard has no tail," Debbie explained. "She's going to die."

"She just lost her tail. Lizards do that when they're scared. It's called predator avoidance. The enemy goes after the tail and the lizard hides. The tail grows back." Riley held Megarra near Debbie's face. Debbie touched her finger with a plain, stubby nail to Meg's head. She stroked her skin.

"She's really soft, isn't she? I thought she'd be slimy."

"Do you want to hold her?" Riley lifted Meg off his arm for Debbie.

"No, no, that's okay." Debbie waved her hands. Her shoulders shivered. "She's probably had enough trauma for one day."

"Grub's on in ten minutes!" Dan knocked on the door.

"Good. I'm so hungry," Debbie said. "I could almost eat crickets."

"They're pretty crunchy actually."

"Have you eaten a cricket?"

"I tried one," Riley said. "They eat them in Africa all the time. I cooked it and everything, though." Debbie's face twisted in disgust.

"It wasn't that bad, really. I just wanted to know what my lizards were tasting."

"You know, I've developed a new admiration for you." Debbie smiled. "Each time I think I've got you figured out, you come out with something new. You're willing to try just about anything."

That's what Mom told Keene the last time Riley was there. "Riley is so adaptable," she'd said. "He'll try any of my food, listen to any of my music, go anywhere I want to go."

Of course I would, Riley thought. I'd do anything to be with Mom. Meg squirmed in Riley's fist; she wanted to be let go.

"You don't like lizards, do you?" Riley lifted the lid and laid Meg on the sunning rock in the tank.

"I didn't hide that very well, did I?" Debbie hugged her knees.

"But you like gophers, don't you?" Riley looked out the window. He could see the flames of the campfire shooting into the dark.

"No. Gophers, lizards, mice, snakes, bugs—anything smaller than a cat gives me the creeps." Debbie's laughter mixed with the loons calling on the lake. *Ew hoooo, ew ew hoooo.*

"But why did we go to the gopher museum?" Riley didn't understand Debbie. Why did she go somewhere she didn't want to go?

"I thought you would like it. That you would think I was great because I took you there." Debbie ran her thumbnail over her other fingernails, chipping away the last of the chocolate polish.

"You're not mad at me about the lizard?" she asked.

"No." He could be mad at other things, but he was the one who'd left the lid off the cage.

"How about the gopher museum?" Debbie rested her chin on her knees. Her bottom lip disappeared between her teeth as she chewed.

"Well, maybe a little." Riley rubbed his arm. He wondered if she'd grab him again, if she got mad enough.

"Yeah, I'm still sort of mad, too." Debbie's words stirred the air. Riley had forgotten how rude he'd been to the museum lady, how he'd been really mad at Debbie then. And mad at everything else,

61

too. It probably wasn't fair, the way he'd acted.

"Thanks for letting me reel in Big Stella. Are you mad that I let her go? I was going to ask but you were too far away."

"No. I'm just glad something worked out. You wanted to catch Big Stella and you caught her." Debbie smiled. She ran her hand through her hair, fluffing it out and then rested her arm on Riley's shoulder in a half-hug.

"It did work out. This was the best day." Riley breathed in Debbie's perfume and campfire-smoke smell all mixed up.

Riley peered into the lizard cage. Lizzy and Megarra were side by side on the sunning rock, green as the evergreen tree Dan had showed Riley on the island where Mom and Dad got married. They'd planted it on their wedding day and now it was twice as tall as Riley and deep forest green.

It looked like it would never die.

Riley watched Megarra slip under the plant, her favorite spot.

He closed his eyes and rested his head on Debbie's shoulder. The lizards weren't scared anymore.

About the Author

Storyteller Mar'ce Merrell draws inspiration from her
household of five children, sometimes as an active
participant in their adventures, sometimes as an observer.
Their real-life dramas combine with the remembered
experiences of her own childhood to fuel her writing.

In addition to storytelling stints at Jasper Park Lodge
and Fort Edmonton Park, writing workshop presen-
tations and author readings take Mar'ce to schools and
conferences throughout Alberta. She says her focus is to
entertain and encourage young writers to create stories
that sing with passion and originality. In *Trading Riley* she
accomplishes just that!